The Dragonsitter's Surprise

First published in 2018 by
Andersen Press Limited
20 Vauxhall Bridge Road
London SW1V 2SA
www.andersenpress.co.uk

2 4 6 8 10 9 7 5 3 1

British Library Cataloguing in Publication Data available.

ISBN 978 1 78344 623 0

Printed and bound in Great Britain by
Clays Limited, Bungay, Suffolk, NR35 1ED

The Dragonsitter's Surprise

Josh Lacey

Illustrated by Garry Parsons

Andersen Press
London

From: Edward Smith-Pickle

To: Morton Pickle

Date: Monday 10 July

Subject: Very exciting news!

Attachments: The egg

Dear Uncle Morton

Do you remember the egg?

I mean the one you gave me for my birthday.

You said it was dead, but you were wrong.

Look at this picture and you'll see why.

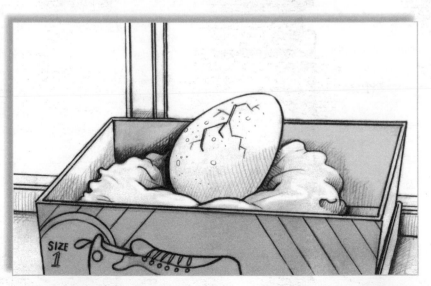

I have already prepared some nice cold sausages and a bar of milk chocolate for the baby dragon's arrival.

I can't wait to see it!

Mum wants to put the egg at the end of the garden till it hatches. She and Gordon spent ages cleaning the house, and they don't want it all messed up.

But what if the baby comes out and gets eaten by one of the cats from next door?

For now I've left it on the windowsill in my bedroom. I hope it will be safe there.

Love from

your favourite nephew

Eddie

Dear Eddie,

Thank you for the delightful photo, but don't get your hopes up.

That egg is dead.

If there is a baby dragon inside, very sadly it will be dead too.

I bought that egg many years ago in a noodle restaurant behind Ulaanbaatar's main railway station.

The chef was planning to use it to make chow mein, but he let me buy it instead. The egg was dead then, and cannot have come alive since.

I can imagine how surprised you were to find a crack in the shell, but sunlight or a sudden change in temperature must have caused that particular fissure.

Please send my best wishes to Emily and the rest of your family. I hope your mother and Gordon are enjoying married life.

Things are busy here. I am hard at work preparing for my expedition to Uzbekistan. I shall be flying over the mountains in a hot air balloon, searching for unicorns.

Would you like to come with me?

With love from

your affectionate uncle

Morton

Dear Uncle Morton

I know you're the expert on dragons, but even so, I think you must be wrong about this egg.

It's now covered in cracks.

Mum swears she hasn't touched it.

Gordon was doing DIY over the weekend, but I don't think an egg could be woken up by the sound of hammering.

Emily says she hasn't even been in my room since last Friday.

There is only one possible explanation. The baby is on its way.

Love from

Eddie

PS Thank you for the invitation, but Mum says I'm not allowed in a hot air balloon and visiting Uzbekistan is out of the question. Which is a pity, because I would really like to see a unicorn.

Dear Uncle Morton

Could you bring your dragons to our house? I need Ziggy's help. And Arthur might be useful too.

The egg is going crazy. Every few minutes it shakes and judders and jiggles. Whatever is inside must be coming out soon.

When the baby arrives, it's going to need a mother.

I asked Mum if she could help, but she said she's got her work cut out already.

Also she's a bit under the weather. She ate a dodgy sandwich the other day, and she's had a funny tummy ever since.

Dear Uncle Morton

The baby is here!

The egg broke open just after breakfast.

Luckily it's the weekend or I would have been getting ready for school. Instead I was playing with Lego when I heard a strange squawk.

I looked up. There on my windowsill was the egg, broken in half.

And there was the baby.

It squawked again. Then it jumped off the windowsill and fluttered its wings.

Unfortunately it doesn't know how to fly yet, so it dropped straight to the floor and landed with a bump.

I picked it up and took it downstairs to show the others.

Arthur was quite small when he was born, but this baby dragon is absolutely tiny.

It doesn't look much like Arthur did.

In fact it doesn't look much like a dragon at all.

For one thing, it's not green. It's yellow. It does have wings, but they're thin and feathery.

Maybe it'll grow more dragony when it's older.

Emily says it's the cutest thing she's ever seen.

Even Gordon thinks it's sweet.

Only Mum doesn't like it. But she's in a grump because she's still feeling sick. I just hope the baby doesn't catch her tummy bug.

We do have one problem. Emily wants to call it Twinkletoes.

I explained that Twinkletoes isn't an appropriate name for a dragon, but Emily won't listen.

You know what little sisters are like. Sometimes they think they're right about everything.

Can you think of a better name?

If you can, please tell me ASAP or this poor dragon will be stuck with Twinkletoes for ever.

Love from

Eddie

Dear Eddie

I am on my way.

I'm leaving for the station right now. Then I shall catch the first train south. With any luck I should be with you tonight.

Until I get there, DO NOT TOUCH THE BABY!

From your photo and your description, I believe she isn't a dragon at all. She sounds more like the Yellow Phoenix.

As I am sure you will remember from my book, the Yellow Phoenix is EXCEEDINGLY DANGEROUS. For more details see page 272 of the copy that I gave you.

If she really is the Yellow Phoenix, she will eat you for breakfast.

I mean that literally.

Morton

Dragons have many enemies, but there is no other creature that they hate as much as the Yellow Phoenix.

An eagle-like bird with fierce talons and a curved beak, the Yellow Phoenix is a rare creature which has never been photographed or even seen by modern scientists. Some legends say she lives for a hundred years; others suggest she lives for only two or three weeks. Some claim she has a brood of ten babies, while others say she lays a single egg from which the next of her kind will be born.

Although neither large nor formidable in appearance, the Yellow Phoenix is famously ruthless and cruel, murdering not only calves and lambs, but donkeys, horses, cattle, and even fully-grown men. In the bleak mountains bordering southern

Mongolia and northern China, I have witnessed otherwise fearless hunters and shepherds speak her name in a whisper, not wanting to curse themselves with bad luck by offending her.

No one knows why the phoenix and the dragon should be such fierce enemies. The origin of their feud is lost in the mists of time. But there is no doubt that terrible battles have been reported between these two species for many centuries, going back as far as the time of Confucius.

According to Ganbaataryn Baast, professor of Zoology at the University of Ulaanbaatar, ancient Mongolian legends suggest that dragons can sense the arrival of a new phoenix, and will attempt to destroy the fledgling before it gains enough strength to defend itself.

Dear Uncle Morton

I don't think Twinkletoes is the Yellow Phoenix.

I looked up page 272 of your book, and your description doesn't sound like her at all.

She might be yellow, but she isn't fierce, let alone ruthless or cruel.

Also she hasn't eaten me for breakfast, although she did steal some of my Coco Pops.

I told Emily not to touch her just in case, but she took absolutely no notice. Instead she picked up Twinkle and refused to put her down.

I warned Emily she might get eaten, but she said she didn't care.

Sometimes little sisters can be so annoying.

I hope you'll have a serious talk with her when you arrive.

Mum says do you want to stay the night?

She says if you do, could you babysit? She and Gordon would like to go to the movies.

Love from

Eddie

From: Edward Smith-Pickle

To: Morton Pickle

Date: Monday 17 July

Subject: Your dragons

Attachments: Unexpected guests

Dear Uncle Morton

We're all a bit confused. You aren't here –
but Ziggy and Arthur are.

They flew onto the patio while we were
having breakfast, and marched straight
through the French windows to say hello.

Are they here to protect us from Twinkle?

If so, they're not doing a very good job.
They took one look at her and ran back
outside.

Now they're sheltering behind some bushes
at the end of the garden.

If I didn't know them better, I'd think they
were scared.

I'll buy them some Maltesers on the way
home from school. I'm sure that will cheer
them up.

Love from

Eddie

Dear Eddie

I am so pleased to learn that Ziggy and Arthur are safely at your house. I have spent the entire weekend searching for them. I couldn't leave my island until I knew they were safe.

Of course Ziggy is more than capable of looking after herself, but I worried that Arthur might have fallen in the sea or lost himself in the sinking sands on the north shore.

They must have come to protect you from the Yellow Phoenix. The legends are clearly correct. Somehow they can sense her presence, even from many miles away.

I am not surprised to hear that they are scared of her. Even the largest dragons are said to fear the Yellow Phoenix, and my two dragons are both quite small.

I shall catch the first train tomorrow morning. Until then: be careful! The phoenix may appear friendly, but it could turn nasty at any moment.

I can't imagine why I gave you an egg as a birthday present. I should have left it in that noodle restaurant.

Oh, and please tell your mother that I am, of course, more than happy to babysit tomorrow night.

Morton

Dear Uncle Morton

Something very strange has happened.
Another dragon arrived in the night.

This one is even bigger than Ziggy. It has
cruel eyes and sharp claws, which have done
terrible damage to Mum's vegetable patch.

I don't know what it's doing here.

The three dragons only come into the house
when Twinkle is upstairs in Emily's bedroom.
But they rush straight outside again as soon
as she comes downstairs.

It's all very mysterious.

Perhaps you're right and Twinkle really is
the Yellow Phoenix. She has grown bigger

and stronger, and she can fly now, but she doesn't look any more like a dragon.

I hope you'll be able to explain everything when you arrive.

Mum says thank you for agreeing to babysit. She and Gordon are really looking forward to the movie. They've booked VIP seats.

Mum's got a chicken pie out of the freezer for our supper, so you'll just have to heat it up. I can show you how to switch on the microwave if you've never used one before.

See you later!

Eddie

Dear Uncle Morton

Where are you?

Mum and Gordon say the movie starts in fifteen minutes, and they'll probably miss the beginning even if they leave right now.

Please get here soon!

Mum's in a bad mood anyway, because Twinkle made a terrible mess today.

Gordon has been doing DIY since he moved in after the wedding. He even mended the shower.

Now the shower's broken again.

Twinkle attacked it this morning. I don't know why. Maybe she thought it was a big silver snake.

Mum wants you to pay for a new shower, a new shower curtain, two new taps, and thirty-three new tiles.

I know the egg is really mine, so I should pay for Twinkle's damage, but I've already spent all my pocket money on Maltesers.

Eddie

From: Edward Smith-Pickle

To: Morton Pickle

Date: Wednesday 19 July

Subject: More dragons

Attachments: Garden party

Dear Uncle Morton

Two more dragons arrived last night.

They're in our garden right now.

Mum says she doesn't know what the neighbours must think.

Mr Braithwaite makes a terrible fuss if I kick a ball into his garden, so he's sure to be furious when he sees five dragons breathing fire all over the place.

One of them did a poo in the middle of the patio, and Mum says I have to clear it up.

I don't see why. I didn't do it.

But she says these stupid dragons are my fault, so if anyone is going to clear up their mess, it has to be me.

29

I think she's still cross about last night. Apparently the VIP seats were very expensive, and they couldn't get a refund.

Was your train delayed? Or cancelled?

Gordon volunteered to come and fetch you, but he doesn't know where you are.

I hope you get here soon. I'm a bit worried about these dragons.

Eddie

Dear Uncle Morton

Another is here! There are now six in our garden.

Dragons, I mean.

Six.

That is a lot of dragons. Especially in a quite small garden.

Mrs Kapelski looked over the fence and said, are we making a film?

I said yes.

Mrs Kapelski said her nephew was an extra in one of the James Bond films and you can see him if you pause it.

31

Mum says Mrs Kapelski isn't all there.

Which is probably a good thing, because if she was, she would have made more fuss about the dragons.

Mr Braithwaite hasn't said anything yet, but I can see him watching through his window. He doesn't look happy.

The neighbours aren't our only problem.

The dragons keep coming into the house and trying to attack Twinkle.

Luckily she's very fast.

Luckily for her, anyway. But not so luckily for our furniture.

One of the dragons missed Twinkle and set the sofa on fire instead.

Another blew up the TV.

There are burn marks all over the ceiling.

If this carries on, there won't be much left of our house.

Eddie

Dear Uncle Morton

Today is the first day of the holidays. I should be enjoying myself.

Instead I've been shovelling poo.

That is not how I want to spend my summer.

Mum says this whole thing is my fault, so I can deal with the consequences.

But I don't see why it's my fault if six dragons decide to live in our garden.

Emily is no help. She just sits in her bedroom with Twinkle, watching me through the window.

Gordon did offer to give me a hand, but Mum wouldn't let him. She said it's a learning experience.

I don't know what I'm meant to be learning.

Except dragon poo is very smelly, and I could have told you that already.

Eddie

Dear Uncle Morton

There are now SEVEN dragons in our garden.

Mum says this is beyond a joke, and I think she might be right.

Poor Twinkle is exhausted. She has to spend all her time fighting dragons, which can't be much fun when you're only one week old.

A man from the council came round this afternoon. He said they've had complaints about excessive noise coming from our house.

I explained we have seven dragons in our back garden and a phoenix sleeping in my sister's bed, so it's no surprise there's a bit of extra noise.

He said all families get rowdy at times, but that's no excuse for disturbing the neighbours.

I invited him to come and see the dragons and the phoenix for himself, but he said he wasn't allowed to cross the threshold without prior permission from the householder.

I said I was the householder, but he said according to regulations the householder has to be at least eighteen years old, and could I please fetch a responsible adult.

Unfortunately Gordon had gone to buy a new drill, and Mum was upstairs in bed. She's feeling sick again.

She says she must have eaten another dodgy sandwich, but I know what the problem really is.

It's the dragons. She's had enough of them. To be honest, Uncle Morton, I have too.

Eddie

From: Morton Pickle

To: Edward Smith-Pickle

Date: Saturday 22 July

Subject: Re: Excessive noise

Attachments: My injuries

Dear Eddie

I am terribly sorry. On Tuesday morning I rowed from my island to the mainland to catch the train. As I was tying my boat to the quay, I tripped on a loose plank, toppled forwards, and knocked myself out. By a stroke of good fortune Mr McDougall happened to witness my predicament and took me directly to A&E.

My head is now wreathed in bandages and the doctors have advised me not to undertake any travel in the immediate future.

39

Of course I am intending to ignore their advice. As soon as I can slip out of hospital, I shall make my way to the train station. I cannot resist the chance to see seven dragons at once. This is literally a once-in-a-lifetime opportunity.

Morton

From: Edward Smith–Pickle
To: Morton Pickle
Date: Sunday 23 July
Subject: Surprise
Attachments: Fight!

Dear Uncle Morton

I have a surprise for you.

It's not actually my surprise. It's Mum's.

It really is very surprising.

She only told us because of the seven dragons.

One of them was trying to get into the house. It might have been hungry. Or it was trying to attack Twinkle. Anyway, it was sneaking through the patio doors when Mum attacked it with a broom.

The dragon reared up its head, and breathed out a great gush of fire, and made a big black mark along the wall, and probably would have fried Mum too if Gordon hadn't thrown a saucepan of water over it.

The dragon wasn't very happy about that.

There was steam everywhere and some terrible shrieking.

The dragon turned and fixed its eyes on Gordon. Then it opened its mouth. I think it was about to eat him alive.

Luckily Twinkle chose that moment to attack the dragon herself.

There was a lot more screaming and shrieking, which only stopped when Gordon pushed the dragon outside and shut the patio doors.

Gordon said married life wasn't meant to be like this. Then he suggested we stay in a hotel till the dragons have gone.

Mum said it's ridiculous paying good money for a hotel when we've got our own house.

Gordon said some things are more important than money.

Mum said, like what exactly?

Gordon said, "A woman in your condition shouldn't have to deal with all this."

As soon as those words left his mouth, he turned bright pink.

So did Mum.

Then they both looked at me and Emily.

There was a long silence. I didn't understand what was going on. I'm sure Emily didn't either.

Mum said, "Gordon and I have got something to tell you."

Gordon said, "Perhaps we'd better sit down."

So we all sat down. Then Mum told us her surprise.

It was worse than I'd expected.

Much, much worse.

She's having a baby.

With Gordon.

I don't want another little sister. One is more than enough.

Mum said it might be a brother, but I don't want one of them either.

I like our family how it is.

Also we only have three bedrooms. Where is this new baby supposed to sleep?

I told Mum I wasn't going to share, and she said: "We'll see."

I know what that means.

I can't share a room with Emily. I just can't.

Can I come and live with you instead?

Love from

Eddie

From: Edward Smith–Pickle

To: Morton Pickle

Date: Monday 24 July

Subject: Formal warning

Attachments: Crazy; Bedroom devastation

Dear Uncle Morton

This is the worst summer holiday of my entire life.

Not just because of the new baby who is going to steal my room. Also because of the dragons.

Normally there's nothing I like more than dragons, but seven is just too many.

They've been going crazy.

They're out in the garden, flapping their wings and stomping their paws and breathing fire and making all sorts of strange noises.

I don't know what's wrong with them.

To be honest, I'm feeling a bit crazy too.

Today four of the dragons flew in through Emily's bedroom window and chased Twinkle round the house.

She tried to hide in my bedroom, but they found her in about two seconds.

There's not much left of my Lego.

Not unless you want a big lump of burnt plastic.

Also three of my posters went up in flames. And my football exploded. And my favourite T-shirt isn't even a T-shirt any more. It's just a bit of burnt cloth.

I'm sorry to say this, Uncle Morton, but I've really had enough of these dragons.

I'm not the only one.

The man from the council came back today. He delivered a formal warning. Now he wants us to pay a fine.

Mum says you'll have to pay it.

She also says the dragons had better leave ASAP or she can't answer for the consequences.

I don't know exactly what she means, but I don't think it's anything nice.

Eddie

Dear Uncle Morton

Today we had a family conference.

Do you know what that is?

I didn't, but apparently it means you all sit around and talk about your feelings.

First we talked about the baby. Mum and Gordon said they can understand why we're worried.

Emily said actually she's not worried and she can't wait for the baby to arrive, because babies are so cute.

I said I am quite worried, because I don't want to share a room with Emily.

That was when Mum and Gordon told us another surprise. We're going to move house! Maybe even to Scotland near you.

Wouldn't that be nice?

We'll all have our own rooms. Even the baby.

And we'll be able to come and see you whenever we want.

Now we just have to persuade the dragons to go away.

Mum says no one will buy a house with seven dragons in the garden, and I'm sure she's right.

The problem is how to make them.

I know your head must be hurting, but do you have any brilliant ideas?

Eddie

From: Morton Pickle

To: Edward Smith–Pickle

Date: Wednesday 26 July

Subject: Re: Conference

Attachments: Room with a view

Dear Eddie

Don't worry. I shall be there very soon.

First I just have to escape from this hospital. It's worse than a prison. I have tried to run away several times, but the nurses keep catching me and bringing me back to my bed.

I shall find a way out. Just give me a little more time.

Until I get there, please don't let the dragons leave.

I am desperate to see them.

I have never seen more than four dragons in the same place at the same time, and that was in a very dark cave.

Morton

PS Please send my congratulations to Gordon and your mother.

Dear Uncle Morton

I'm very sorry, but you are going to be too late to see the dragons.

They just left.

It was my fault. I'm sorry.

I've also done something even worse.

I've killed Twinkletoes.

I feel awful.

I thought I was being clever. I had this brilliant idea. I thought if I took Twinkle outside, the dragons would get frightened, and they'd all fly away.

Holding her in my hands, I took her into the garden.

Emily tried to stop me. She said the dragons would try to kill Twinkle and probably me too.

I took no notice.

But she was right.

I stepped out on to the patio and held Twinkle in the air and showed her to the dragons.

I thought they'd fly away. Or at least run down to the end of the garden.

Instead they charged at me.

All seven at once.

It was really scary.

Ziggy and Arthur are usually so nice and friendly, but this time they were terrifying.

All I could see was teeth and smoke.

I really thought I was going to get burnt to death.

But Twinkle saved me. She flapped her wings and wriggled out of my hands and flew straight at the dragons.

There were seven of them, and only one of her.

They were huge, and she's tiny.

I thought she wouldn't have a chance.

But she fought like a tiger. A tiger with wings.

The battle seemed to last for hours, but it couldn't have been more than a minute or two. Then all seven dragons turned on Twinkle and breathed fire at the same moment.

The heat was amazing. Twinkle actually seemed to explode into flames.

Even the dragons were surprised. They all jumped back in amazement.

Luckily Emily and I did too. Otherwise we would have been burnt alive.

Even so we both lost quite a lot of hair.

When we opened our eyes, the grass was smouldering. Not much was left of the tree except some blackened branches. And Twinkle had been burnt to a crisp.

There was literally nothing left of her.

Just a big pile of ashes and soot and bits of burnt stuff.

The dragons left after that. They flew away without even saying goodbye. Or thanks for all the Maltesers.

I'm sorry, Uncle Morton. I know how much you wanted to see all the dragons. And the phoenix too.

Emily cried for a bit, but she's cheered up now, because she and Mum have been going through her old baby clothes, deciding which ones are worth keeping.

Gordon has gone to buy pickled onions and strawberry ice cream. Apparently that's what Mum wants for lunch.

No wonder she's been feeling sick.

Love from

Eddie

Dear Eddie

I'm so sorry that the dragons have gone. I wish you could have kept them in your house for just one more day. But don't blame yourself. Dragons and the Yellow Phoenix have an enmity as old as time, and your own efforts, however valiant, could never have ended the conflict between those ancient foes.

As soon as I got your last message, I realised there was no reason to come south. Instead I returned home – and can you guess what I found in the garden?

That's right: Ziggy and Arthur. Fast asleep on the grass. They must have been exhausted from their long flight.

I have a large snack awaiting them when they wake up.

Both my dragons are covered in cuts and bruises. I suppose they must have hurt themselves during their battle with the Yellow Phoenix. But they both seem to be sleeping contentedly.

With love from

your affectionate uncle

Morton

PS Perhaps you should go into the garden and search through the ashes of that bonfire. You know what they say about phoenixes!

From: Edward Smith–Pickle

To: Morton Pickle

Date: Friday 28 July

Subject: What they say

Attachments: Egg

Dear Uncle Morton

I was a bit confused by your last message, because I didn't know what they say about phoenixes.

But I looked them up, and now I do.

I went into the garden and had a look around.

And you were right!

I searched the lawn and the bushes and Mum's vegetable patch. At first there didn't seem to be anything except charred leaves and burnt twigs and black dirt.

Then I found it.

An egg.

Just like the last one.

I brought it indoors, and wrapped it up safely in bubble wrap. Then I put it in a box.

This afternoon Mum wanted a bit of peace and quiet, so Gordon took us shopping.

First we bought some more paint.

Gordon has to repaint all the walls before we can even ring any estate agents. No one wants to buy a house with burn marks on the ceiling.

Then we went to the post office.

I liked having Twinkletoes living with us, but I think Mum and Gordon are right. The house is going to be crowded enough already.

So I've sent you the egg.

Love from

Eddie

From: Professor Ganbaataryn Baast

To: Morton Pickle

Date: Tuesday 8 August

Subject: Phoenix

Attachments: Egg; Zoology laboratory

My dear Morton

Greetings from Ulaanbaatar!

I hope you are very well and the weather in Scotland is fine for the time of year.

Here in Mongolia we have been treated to much sunshine. I just wish I had more time to enjoy it!

Thank you for the extraordinary news about the Yellow Phoenix.

As you must remember, I devoted nine years of my life to searching for that elusive creature. I almost died of thirst in the Gobi Desert and nearly froze to death in the Altai Mountains. But I never caught one single glimpse of the Yellow Phoenix.

So I was most impressed and excited to see the wonderful photographs taken by your nephew. Please pass on my thanks to Eddie. He has some chips from the old block, as you say in English.

Please thank him also for the egg. I appreciate the gift very much. It is now stored in perfect conditions in my laboratory.

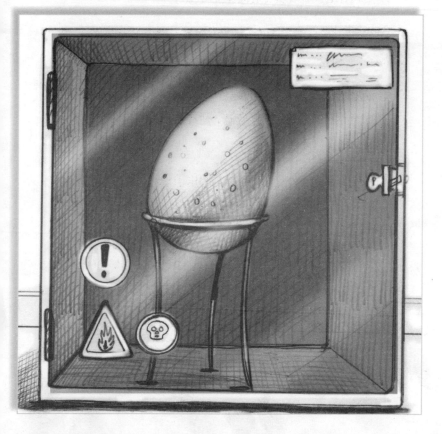

If it hatches, you and your nephew will the first to know.

I hope you will be visiting Ulaanbaatar again soon.

Next year I am hoping to make an expedition to Tavan Bogd, the biggest mountain in our country, and home of many interesting creatures.

With good luck I will be there to see the Great Dragon Battle Ceremony. Please accompany me if you have some free time.

Maybe Eddie will come also? He is very welcome for joining us.

As we say here in Mongolia, my yurt is your yurt.

With best regards,

Gan

Professor Ganbaataryn Baast,
Department of Zoology,
University of Ulaanbaatar,
Mongolia

The Dragonsitter Detective

Josh Lacey

Illustrated by Garry Parsons

Dear Uncle Morton
Are you sitting down? If you're not, you probably should.
Because I have some very bad news. Someone has stolen
one of your dragons.

Eddie's mum is getting remarried in Scotland. But just
before the wedding, Ziggy is stolen. It's not long before
Arthur is taken too. Eddie must track the thief down,
rescue Uncle Morton's dragons and get to the church
on time . . .

'An accessible and fun read'
Carousel

9781783445295   £4.99

So could you please bring Ziggy here ASAP.

I know she isn't really its mother, but she could be its stepmother instead.

Love from

Eddie

From: Morton Pickle
To: Edward Smith–Pickle
Date: Friday 14 July
Subject: Re: Mum needed

Dear Eddie

Don't worry. You are not going to need Ziggy or any other mothers, because that egg is never going to hatch.

I can't imagine what could be causing the cracks, the shakes, the judders, or the jiggles, but there must be some perfectly rational explanation.

Morton